VAMPIRE VACATION

BY
LAURA LAVOIE

ART BY
MICAH PLAYER

VIKING

VIKING
An imprint of Penguin Random House LLC, New York

First published in the United States of America by Viking,
an imprint of Penguin Random House LLC, 2022

Visit us online at penguinrandomhouse.com.

Library of Congress Cataloging-in-Publication Data is available.

Manufactured in Spain

ISBN 9780593203132

1 3 5 7 9 10 8 6 4 2

EST

Design by Opal Roengchai
Text set in Superclarendon
The illustrations were created in Adobe Photoshop on a Surface Studio 2.

For Phil, Lilah, and Violet
—L. L.

To Simon, who loves the sea
—M. P.

Fang was not your everyday vampire.

Coffin carving? Yawn!

So when Mama and Papa planned
another family trip to Transylvania,
Fang decided to drop some hints.

"Look! I can hang ten!"

"Jumping jellyfish! I spy a stingray!"

"Don't worry, it's safe with SPF five thousand!"

Mama rubbed her eyes.
"Why are you awake in
the middle of the day?
What's gotten into you?!"

"I want to go to the beach! All my friends go, and it looks like so much fun. See?"

"I don't care what ghosts, mummies, and witches do," said Papa. "Vampires vacation in Transylvania."

"But we always do the same things," Fang complained.

"Nonsense," said Papa. "It will be fun! We'll tour Dracula's castle, visit the House of No Mirrors, dine at a five-star blood bank . . ."

"I've got to convince them," Fang told Ambrosia. "I was *born* to build sandcastles! I'm *destined* to surf! I'd rather *eat garlic* than go on another trip to Transylvania!"

Before family movie night, Fang stormed the library, searched the film collection, and selected the perfect flick.

"Look how fun this would be!"

"AHHHHHH!" Mama shrieked.
"Is that a *stake*?"

"Vampires don't scuba dive!" said Papa.

Fang's shoulders slumped.
"Okay, Ambrosia. New plan.
I'll show Mama and Papa the beach isn't scary."

He shopped for supplies, rallied the troops,
and announced a family fashion show.

"Look how cute they are!"

Papa shook his head.
"Vampires don't sport swimwear."

"Take off those flippers," said Mama.
"It's almost coffintime."

Fang buried his face
in his hands.

"Why won't they listen? I need to do something big . . .

HUGE . . .

COLOSSAL!

If they won't go to the beach, I'll bring the beach to them!

"Sand? Check!

"Seashells?
Check!

"Seagulls?
Err . . . check!

"Time to decorate Papa's Man Cave!"

"Fang Vladimir Bloodgood the Third! What is this mess?!"

Fang hung his head. "I wanted to show you how much fun the beach could be. I'm sorry!"

Mama wrapped him in a hug.
"We'll talk about this later.
Right now, let's clean up."

Fang helped clean up the Cave.

He sulked,

sniffled,

then sobbed,

"I'll n-n-never feel the salty
ocean breeze in my h-h-hair!"

Mama sighed. "You know, I've always thought about touring the Black Sea caves . . ."

"I *have* wanted time to practice my batminton game . . ."

"Look," said Fang, "they're making sand phantoms."

Mama and Papa shared a look.
"I suppose we could *try* a beach vacation . . ."

"REALLY?!"
Fang sprinted to pack.

"First up: sandcastles!

"Now: snorkeling!

"Big finale: surfing!

"This is the best vacation EVER!"

"I have to admit," said Mama, "I love my new flip-flops!"

"You were right, Fang," Papa agreed. "This *is* better than another trip to Transylvania."

"You know, I have some ideas for
other new things we could try . . .

"Have you ever heard of tobogganing?
Or snowboarding? Or dogsled rides?!"